CIRCUS FAMILY DOG

CIRCUS FAMILY DOG

by **ANDREW CLEMENTS**

illustrated by **SUE TRUESDELL**

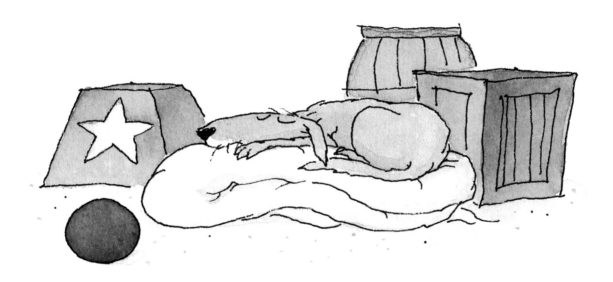

Clarion Books • New York

Clarion Books
a Houghton Mifflin Company imprint
215 Park Avenue South, New York, NY 10003
Text copyright © 2000 by Andrew Clements
Illustrations copyright © 2000 by Sue Truesdell
First Clarion paperback edition, 2008.

The text was set in 17-point Calisto.
The illustrations were executed in watercolor and pen-and-ink.

www.clarionbooks.com

Manufactured in China

The Library of Congress has cataloged the hardcover edition as follows:
Clements, Andrew, 1949–
Circus family dog / by Andrew Clements ; illustrated by Sue Truesdell.
p.   cm. Summary: Grumps is content to do his one trick in the center ring at the circus,
until a new dog shows up and steals the show—temporarily.
ISBN: 0-395-78648-7
[1. Dogs—Fiction. 2. Circus—Fiction.] I. Truesdell, Sue, ill. II. Title
PZ7.C59118 Ci   2000
[E] 21   99052657

CL ISBN–13: 978-0-395-78648-2
PA ISBN–13: 978-0-547-01639-9

WKT 10 9 8 7 6 5 4 3 2 1

For my family near and far, the greatest show on earth
—A.C.

For Erica
—S.T.

The circus is like a family,
and old Grumps was the family dog.

7

The show traveled from town to town.
Each night under the Big Top,
the clowns came rushing in.
Out in the center ring,
Red the Clown lit the flaming hoop.
There was a drum roll,
and the audience shushed and hushed.
The clowns yelled,
"Come on, Grumps, you can do it, boy!
Jump! Jump!"

Grumps looked up at the hoop
and crouched low.

And then he yawned,
and closed his eyes,
and lay down with his feet up in the air.

That was his trick—his one and only trick.
The children loved it.

The clowns yelled and pushed and pulled
until the old dog was back up on his feet.

When Grumps yawned, and closed his eyes,
and lay down AGAIN with his feet up in the air,
the children laughed and pointed and screamed,
"Jump, Grumps! Jump!"

Then, while everyone clapped and cheered,
the clowns laid Grumps on his wagon
and pulled him slowly out of the Big Top.
And the old circus dog was happy.

One day Red the Clown brought a new dog
into the Big Top.
His name was Sparks.

Sparks could balance
a ball
on
his
nose.

Sparks could climb
a ladder
on
his
hind feet.

Sparks could ride
on the back of a running zebra.

And one night out in the center ring,
when Grumps lay down with his feet in the air,
Sparks jumped right over Grumps,
up and through the burning hoop.

"Hurray for Sparks! Hurray for Sparks!"
the children screamed. Every night the audience
laughed and cheered for Sparks.

And every night the clowns laid Grumps on his wagon
and pulled him from the ring.
But Grumps wasn't happy.
He was miserable.

Out behind the tents Grumps worked day after day.

He ran at the hoop
and banged his nose.

He jumped at the hoop
and bonked his head.

He threw himself into the hoop
and scraped his belly.

At night out in the center ring,
Grumps yawned, and closed his eyes,
and lay down with his feet up in the air.
It felt so good to flop down on the sawdust.

His bones ached and his eyes watered.
He was too tired to care when Sparks
jumped over him.

But each day, Grumps kept on working.

The last day of the State Fair
was the biggest show of the year.

The clowns came rushing into the tent,
and out into the center ring.
Red the Clown lit the flaming hoop.
There was a drum roll,
and the audience shushed and hushed.

The clowns yelled,
"Come on, Grumps, you can do it, boy!
Jump! Jump!"
Grumps did his trick
—his one and only trick.
Then Sparks leaped up over Grumps,
up and through the burning hoop.
"Hurray for Sparks! Hurray for Sparks!"

The trick was over,
and Red the Clown leaned over
to pat Sparks on the head.
But the trick wasn't over—not tonight.

Grumps slowly stood up and took three steps back.

He crouched

and ran
and jumped—

up and in and through the flaming hoop,

and he landed right on Red the Clown.
Down went Red,
and down went Sparks,
in a jumble of paws and wigs
and floppy clown shoes.

The crowd cheered,
and Grumps stood there in the spotlight—
panting and bruised and aching all over,
but happy.
Red stood up, and he clapped too.
And Sparks wagged his tail.

The circus moved on.
There were more shows in other towns,
but old Grumps never jumped through the
flaming hoop again.

Yet every single night, Grumps got his fair share
of the smiles and the cheers—
Red the Clown and Sparks made sure that he did.
Why?

Because the circus is like a family,
and old Grumps was the family dog.